Fables of La Fontaine

Fables of La Fontaine

TRANSLATED BY
LISA COMMAGER
ILLUSTRATED BY
JIŘÍ TRNKA

Exeter Books

NEW YORK

Contents

The grasshopper sang the whole summer long, but when the cold North Wind came along, she got scared. Suddenly she couldn't find even a sliver of fly or a curl of worm to feast on.

Crying from hunger, she went to visit the ant next door. 'Please, dear ant,' she said, 'won't you be so kind as to lend me a tiny bit of grain to get by on until the winter is over? I promise, on my honour as an animal, I'll pay you back the entire amount before August — with interest!'

Now the ant isn't given to lending — you might say lending is the least of her faults. So she asked, 'What were you up to all summer, when it was warm?'

'Oh,' replied the grasshopper, 'I sang, day and night, to give pleasure to all who passed by. Doesn't that make you happy?'

'Sure,' said the ant, 'it makes me very happy to know that, it gives me peace of mind. You sang. That's fine. Now dance.'

Master Crow sat on a tree with a piece of cheese in his beak. Master Fox was passing by, and, attracted by the smell of cheese, he stopped and looked up.

'Ah, Mister Crow!' said he. 'Aren't you looking marvellous today! You really are a handsome fellow. If your singing voice is anything like as fine as those feathers of yours, you must be the greatest bird in this wood!'

At these words, the crow nearly passed out for joy. To show off his gorgeous voice, he opened his beak as far as he could — and the cheese fell out.

The fox picked it up and said, 'My dear friend, you now understand that a flatterer profits at the expense of anyone who is silly enough to listen to his praise. A cheese is a small price to pay for such a lesson, wouldn't you say?'

The crow, humiliated and confused, swore he'd never be tricked again. But it was too late to get his cheese back.

The Frog who Wanted to be as Big as an Ox

Once there was a frog who met an ox. The frog thought the ox was the most beautiful creature she had ever seen. The frog wasn't even as big as an egg, but she longed to be like the ox, so she stretched, and she stretched, and she blew herself up like a balloon.

'Look at me, sister,' she said. 'Is it enough? Am I as big as you? Tell me, am I there?'

'No,' mooed the ox placidly. 'Not yet.'

The frog kept on blowing.

'Am I there now?' she gasped.

'Not remotely there,' said the ox.

The frog stretched and strained even harder.

'And now?' she croaked.

'You don't even begin to make it,' replied the ox.

The poor, paltry little frog kept inflating herself with air until she burst. There was no frog left to admire the ox.

The world is full of people like that. Those who are small want to be big, and those who are big need to have smaller people around them, so they can feel important.

A couple of mules were tramping along the road together. One was carrying two bags of oats, the other was carrying two big bags of silver for taxes. The one with the silver was very proud of himself; he wouldn't change his heavy load for the oats even for a moment. He high-stepped along, slow and fancy as a king, ringing his bells to attract attention to himself.

A gang of thieves came running up to see what all the noise was about. When they saw the mule with those great big bags bulging with what looked like it might be money, they started beating him up.

The mule moaned, and he groaned, and he cried to his friend, 'Is this the kind of treatment I deserve for being so special? All you did was trail along behind me, and you're safe. I'm much more brilliant than you, and they're killing me. Is this justice?'

'Well, if you ask me,' replied the other, 'it isn't always a good idea to have an important job. If you worked for a simple miller as I do, instead of for a tax collector, you wouldn't be in this fix.'

One day, the great god Jupiter called all the
animals together to see if they had any complaints
about the way he had made them.

'Monkey,' said Jupiter, 'you speak first, you're
a sensible fellow. Look around at all these other
animals. Would you like to be more like any of
them?'

'Me?' said the monkey. 'Why would I want to
be different? Don't I have four legs, like everybody
else? Isn't my face as nice as anyone's? Look at my
brother the bear. Compared to me, he's like a rough
sketch compared to a fine oil painting. Who would
ever bother to paint him?'

The bear ambled up and everyone thought she
was going to complain about her ugliness. But she
said, 'I think you should remake the elephant. She
has too short a tail and her ears are too big; she's
a mess of an animal.'

Well, the elephant said the same sort of thing.
She thought the whale was too fat.

The ant said the mite was too skinny to be
attractive, while she herself was a fine figure of an
insect.

Finally, Jupiter sent them all packing back into the woods, criticizing one another and praising themselves.

Aren't people the same, very clever about the faults of others, and blind to their own? And if they do see any faults in themselves — they forgive themselves quickly! It's as though they have two pairs of eyes, one for seeing themselves, the other for looking at others. People are like beggars, who have big baggy coats with two pockets. The back pocket is for their own faults, and the front pocket is for the faults of others.

There was a swallow living in a field who had travelled all around the world, and had learned a great deal. What she learned, she remembered. She could tell when even the smallest storm was brewing, and she always warned sailors if she saw one coming.

The season came for sowing hemp in the field, and the sparrow watched anxiously while a peasant covered the land with deep furrows. 'Listen,' she said to the other birds, who were even smaller than she was and much less experienced, 'you'd better watch out! I'm all right, I can fly away, or curl up in a corner till the danger is over. But you little ones had better be careful. Do you see that huge hand looming over you in the air? Do you know what it means? One day soon, enormous nets will be made out of the hemp that comes from these seeds and those nets will be snares for you. After you're caught, you'll be locked up in cages, or cooked in ovens. So what you must do is eat the seeds. Please listen to me! I know what I'm talking about.'

The little birds laughed at her. How could they possibly eat all those seeds? She was just being silly, they said.

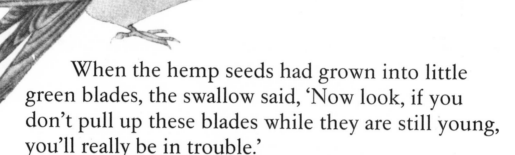

When the hemp seeds had grown into little green blades, the swallow said, 'Now look, if you don't pull up these blades while they are still young, you'll really be in trouble.'

'You gloomy old thing, you're just trying to spoil our fun,' said the birds. 'Nice work you give us! We'd have to be a thousand people to pull up all these blades of hemp! Calm down! Enjoy yourself!'

The hemp soon reached maturity. The swallow said, 'It's a bad sign when the grain is ready so early. Now look, this is your last chance. As soon as the people stop fussing over the grain, they'll make war on us. When they've laid their snares and spread their nets of hemp, for goodness sake, don't flit around from place to place acting like nothing has happened! Either you have to hide, or get out. And yet, you know, you can't leave — you'd never be able to make it across the desert and seas to search for other worlds. You aren't big and strong like the duck and the crane and the woodcock. There's only one thing you can do. Climb into the holes of that wall, and stay there till the danger is past.'

The other birds were bored by the sound of her voice. They started babbling, so they wouldn't have to hear her any more, the way the Trojans did, when poor Cassandra tried to warn them that the Greeks were coming in a wooden horse, long, long ago.

Suddenly, all at once, the birds understood what she was talking about. But by that time, they were already slaves, trapped in the net. Strange, how it never seems possible that anything bad will happen, until it does.

nce there was a poor wolf who was nothing but skin and bones. The guard dogs on the farm were all doing their jobs so well he couldn't get any food. One day, the wolf met one of those dogs, who had somehow gone astray. The dog was as handsome as he was strong. Sir Wolf would willingly have attacked the dog and torn him limb from limb, but the dog was in form to defend himself boldly. So the wolf began to chat with him instead.

'You are wonderfully plump!' he said.

'You could easily be like me if you wanted to,' said the dog. 'All you have to do is to lead a better life. You poor wretches off there in the woods are bound to die of hunger. And for what? Nothing is certain for you. You never get a really good free meal. You are always being hounded and killed. Why don't you join the dogs? You'd have a much better time.'

'That sounds like a great idea,' said the wolf. 'What do I have to do?'

'Almost nothing,' said the dog, 'except chase away a few people with sticks, and some measly beggars. You flatter the people who live in the big house, and you please your master. In return, you

get scraps from their table, chicken bones, pigeon bones, and lots of loving too.'

The wolf's eyes filled with tears as he imagined the bliss that awaited him. He eagerly followed his new friend. Suddenly he noticed that the dog's neck was bare.

'What's wrong with your neck?' he asked. 'There's no hair!'

'Nothing's wrong,' said the dog.

'What do you mean, nothing?'

'Nothing much.'

'What do you mean, nothing much?'

'Maybe the collar I'm usually attached to the chain with is the cause of that little touch of baldness.'

'Attached?' gasped the wolf. 'Do you mean to tell me you can't run about where you want to?'

'Maybe not always, but who cares?'

'I care,' said the wolf. 'All your terrific meals I wouldn't want at that price. I wouldn't trade my freedom for the most precious treasure in the world.' And the wolf ran back into the woods.

ight makes right. I'll tell you what I mean. One day, a lamb was quenching his thirst in a stream when a wolf came along. The wolf hadn't had his breakfast, and he was hungry. When he saw the lamb, he yelled, 'How dare you mess up my water by drinking it? You'll be punished for this!'

'Sire,' replied the lamb, 'please don't be angry. If you will take into your kind consideration the fact that I was drinking more than twenty feet from where your majesty is standing, and that, in consequence, it is quite impossible that I should in any way have disturbed the cleanliness of your highness's drinking water . . .'

'Well, you are disturbing it,' snarled the wolf. 'And besides, I happen to know that you were saying bad things about me behind my back last year.'

'How could I? I wasn't born last year! I'm still at my mother's teat!' said the lamb.

'If it wasn't you, it was your brother.'

'I don't have one!'

'Well, it was one of you lot. You never stop talking about me, you and your shepherds and your dogs. I've heard all about the mean things you say. So now I'm going to get back at you.' Then the wolf carried the sheep to the edge of the forest and ate him, without more ado.

Deep in a primitive cave, a satyr and his family were about to eat their supper. They ate on the moss. They had no rug nor any cloth, but they had good appetites.

A passerby, chilled from the rain, burst in. They had not expected him, but they invited him to share their broth. They didn't need to offer twice.

The first thing he did was to warm his fingers by blowing on them. Then he gently blew on the soup they gave him.

The satyr was astonished. 'For heaven's sake, what good does that do?'

'One breath is to cool down my soup; the other makes my hands warm,' the man explained.

'You can leave right now,' said the primitive half-man. 'The gods would disapprove if I let you remain in my home. I'll stay away from anyone whose breath can blow both hot and cold!'

The elegant fox, with great formality, invited his dear friend the stork to dinner. It wasn't much of meal he served. It was rather small, and didn't look as though it had taken very long to prepare. In fact, there was nothing but clear broth, served up on a very flat plate.

The stork had a long, pointed beak, so of course she couldn't cope with the watery stuff. The sly old fox lapped it up in a moment.

The stork decided she'd get back at the fox for his awful joke. She invited him to her house.

'Why sure,' said the fox, 'I'd be glad to visit you. I'll do anything to make my friends happy.'

At the appointed hour, he ran to the stork's house. Before he even sat down to eat he started praising her for her kind hospitality, and congratulating her on her exquisite cooking. He wished her good appetite: foxes never forget their manners. He rejoiced at the smell of the meat, all cut into tiny pieces which he said were delightfully dainty.

The food was served up in a vase with a long neck and a narrow opening. The beak of the stork could fit into the vase all right, but the nose of the fox was made to another measure.

The fox went home as ashamed as a fox who has been caught by a hen, dragging his tail and drooping his ears. Tricksters, it's to you I'm telling this tale! Don't make a fool of somebody, unless you're willing to look foolish too.

One day, the oak tree said to the reed, 'You should be angry at Nature for making you so puny. A tiny bird is a heavy load for you. The least little breeze that wafts by and wrinkles the face of the water makes you bow your head. Now I'm as vast as a mountain. I not only block the rays of the sun, I stand up to the rage of the tempest. To you, every breath of air is the North Wind; to me, the North Wind is a gentle breath of air.

'If only you'd been born in the shelter of some bushes, with me for your protector, you wouldn't have to suffer so much! I'd defend you against any storm. But you and your kind almost always are found on the humid edges of the realms of wind. Nature seems very cruel to me.'

The reed replied, 'Sir, your compassion does you credit. But do stop worrying. Actually, the winds are less threatening to me than they are to you. I bend, and never break. You have until now resisted the onslaught of every wind without bowing your massive head. But let's wait and see what happens.'

Just as the reed said these words, the most terrible of the children that the North had yet brought forth from her womb came rushing up to them in a fury. The tree stood firm; the reed bent. The wind blew even harder, and did so well, that he uprooted the great tree whose head was neighbour to the sky and whose feet were buried where death lived.

A bat hit her head against a weasel's nest and right away the weasel, who had long been a mouse-hater, rushed to devour her.

'How dare you come within my sight!' screeched the weasel. 'After what your brood has done to me! You are a mouse, aren't you? Tell me the truth! Yes, you're a mouse all right; if you aren't, I'm no weasel.'

'I beg your pardon,' said the bat, 'but mouse is not my profession. Me, a mouse! Some jealous animal must have told you that. Thank God, I am a bird. Look at my wings. Long live the tribe that clings to air!'

Her words impressed the weasel, and he let her go.

Two days later, the bat blindly thrust herself into the home of another weasel, this one a bird-hater. Once again, the bat's life was in danger. The weasel got all ready to crunch her up between her teeth as a bird. The bat started shouting that it was an outrage. 'What do you take me for? Don't you have eyes in your head? What makes a bird?

It's the feathers, right? I am a furry mouse. Long live the mouse family! Down with all cats!' By this kind of talk she saved her life a second time.

Lots of people change their tune when they are in danger. Suddenly they hate what they loved before. According to them, the wise person is one who can say convincingly both 'Long live the king!' and 'Down with the king!'

By his work one knows the worker.

Some honeycombs lay empty, and a bunch of hornets claimed them. The bees said the honeycombs were theirs, so they all took the case to a wasp to settle.

The wasp didn't know what to do, so he called some witnesses, who claimed they'd seen some long-winged, tan insects hanging around the honeycomb making a buzzing noise. The hornets said, 'So, we fit that description as well as the bees do!'

The wasp still didn't know what to do, so he called a new trial, and this time he asked a colony of ants to help decide who was right.

'What's the point of all this, for goodness' sake?' asked a sensible bee. 'For nearly six months this case has droned on, and it's got nowhere. Meanwhile, the honey is going bad. Why can't the judge stop dragging his feet? Let's forget all these objections and interrogations and confusions and obscurities and let the hornets and the bees get to work. Then you'll see who can actually make a syrup so sweet to drink, and cells so lovely to live in.'

The hornets said they thought that was a horrible idea, and of course that gave them away. So the wasp judged the bees the rightful owners of the beehive.

If only all cases could be decided that way! If simple common sense could take the place of legal proceedings, solving problems wouldn't cost so much. The way it is now, so much time and money is eaten up that in the end the judge gets the oyster and the poor citizen, even if he wins his case, gets only the hollow shell.

Mortally wounded by a feathered arrow, a bird mourned for his life. 'Oh, why did I have to give them the means to kill me? Cruel human beings, you pull out our wings to make these weapons to murder us with. But don't mock us. Your time will come! So often, you meet the same fate you inflict on birds. One half of the human race is always busy piling up arms to destroy the other half.'

One day, a cock dug up a beautiful pearl, which he gave to a jeweller who lived nearby. 'I find it very fine,' said the cock, 'but the smallest grain of millet means more to me.'

An ignorant man inherited a splendid manuscript, which he took to his neighbour, the scholar. 'I think it's very good,' said the man to the scholar, 'but even a penny would have more value for me.'

Once upon a time, the town rat invited his dear friend the country rat to come and eat some splendid leftovers at his house. They spread their picnic on a lovely Turkish rug, and settled down to a most glorious party. The food was really special, there was nothing they could have wanted that they didn't have.

But while they were eating, they were suddenly disturbed by a noise at the door. The town rat scurried away to hide, and his comrade scampered after him.

When the noise stopped, the rats rushed back to their food.

'Now we can finish our first course in peace,' said the town rat, looking as casual as he could.

'Thanks, but I've had enough to eat,' said the country rat. 'I'll tell you what, you come and visit me tomorrow. It's not that I don't like your magnificent meal, it's fit for a king. But where I come from, even if the food is not so fancy, I have plenty of time to enjoy it.'

A cat named Rodilard caused so much grief to rats that people never even saw them any more. Rodilard had sent so many rats to their graves, that the few who were left didn't dare leave their houses. They couldn't get nearly enough to eat. Rodilard was considered by the unhappy rats to be not a cat, but a devil. Now one day, that cat went off to find his lady friend, and he stayed out frolicking all night. The rats seized their chance, and held a meeting about what to do.

A very wise old rat suggested that as soon as possible they should attach a bell to the neck of the

cat. That way, he said, when Rodilard was about to pounce they'd hear him, and be able to escape.

Well, all the rats thought that was a wonderful idea. But the problem was, who would attach the bell to the neck of the cat?

One of them said, 'I'm certainly not doing it, I wouldn't be so stupid.'

Another one said, 'I wouldn't begin to know how.'

And so it went. Without doing anything they gave up. I've seen plenty of meetings like that, meetings not of rats, but of people in high positions. Anybody can make decisions. The world is full of people willing to tell you what to do. But to get anything done is a different story.

Scram, you measly insect, you scum of the earth!' When the lion spoke that way to the gnat, the gnat declared war on the lion.

'Do you think,' inquired the gnat, 'that just because you are called king you can scare me, or even get me slightly worried? The ox is tougher than you are, and I can make him do whatever I please.' And he sounded his bugle to call himself to arms. He was both the bugle and the hero. Then he flew all around the lion, taking his time, making a reconnaissance of the territory.

Suddenly he darted into the lion's mane. He nearly drove the great beast mad. The lion frothed at the mouth, and his eyes flashed. He roared, so that animals for miles around trembled and hid. And all that commotion was due to one little gnat. The paltry little creature tormented the lion in a million places, stinging his back, his snout, and creeping even into his nostril.

When that happened, the lion went wild with fury. His invisible enemy sat in his nostril laughing and laughing, knowing the huge creature could never defeat him, with claws, with teeth, with anything.

By this time, the lion had taken to torturing himself, beating his tail against his flanks, pawing the air, until he collapsed from exhaustion. The insect retired in triumph from the field of battle. As he had announced his charge, so now he blasted forth his victory for all the world to hear.

On his grand triumphal march, he encountered a spider's ambush. There he met his end.

What does all this mean? I see two things. First of all, among enemies, the most harmless looking are often the most to be feared. And second, one can survive great dangers, and then be conquered by almost nothing.

The Donkey Loaded with Sponges
and the Donkey Loaded with Salt

A donkey driver, bearing a sceptre like a Roman emperor, led his two long-eared steeds down the road. One, bearing sponges, marched like a fine courier, but the other, weighed down with salt, dragged his feet and lagged behind. These fancy pilgrims made their way over hills and brooks by narrow paths, and finally arrived at the ford of a river. The donkeys felt uneasy. But the driver wasn't worried. He mounted the lively donkey, the one with the sponges, and urged the one with the salt to go ahead.

The donkey with the salt didn't need to be told twice. Seeing his chance to escape, he rushed ahead, and stumbled into a hole. He landed in the water, but managed to get out, because all the salt had dissolved in the stream, and nothing weighed him down any more.

His comrade the sponger followed his example, like a sheep who does whatever the others do. But when he plunged into the water, he and his master and his sponges all got stuck there. You see, the sponges filled with water, until they were so heavy the donkey couldn't budge. His owner clung to him, and they waited for death.

As a matter of fact, somebody came to their rescue. It doesn't matter who, that's not the point of my story. The point is, really, that it's not always a good idea to do exactly what others do.

It is a good idea to be nice to everybody you meet. You often find yourself in need of somebody smaller than you. I'll tell you two stories to show you what I mean, but you can see examples of it everywhere.

A rat recklessly scrambled out of a hole in the field to find himself between the paws of a lion. The king of animals showed his royal nature, and granted the rat his life. The rat never forgot.

But who would imagine that a lion could ever need the help of a little rat?

It happened one day, that as that lion was strolling near the edge of the forest, he got caught in a net. He roared and roared, but he couldn't roar his way out of the net. The rat heard the noise and came running to help his friend. He gnawed away at the net as hard as he could, and eventually, he made a hole big enough for the lion to crawl out. Patience and effort have more power than rage.

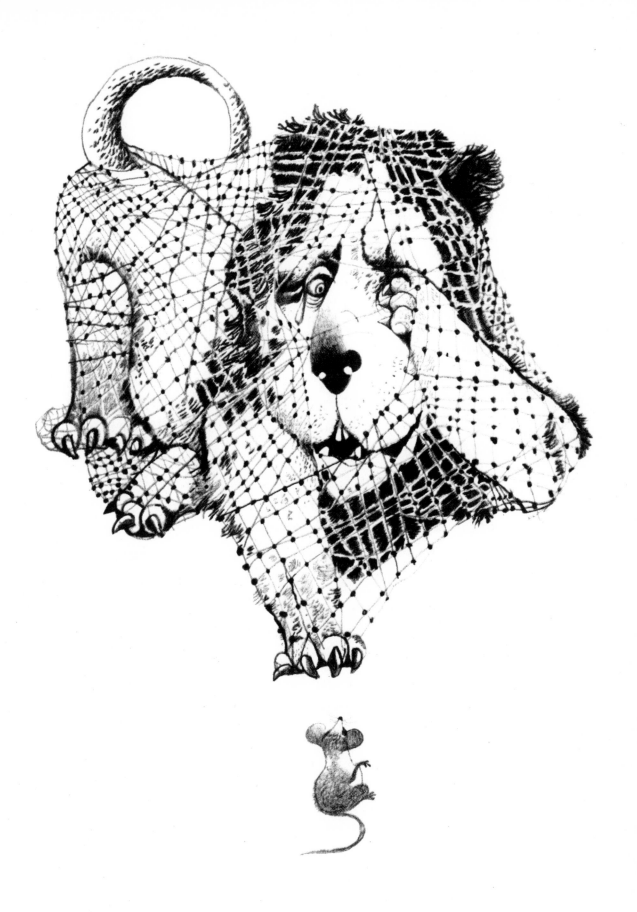

The other story is about smaller animals.

One day, a pigeon was drinking in a clear stream. Suddenly she saw a fly fall into the water. To the fly, the stream was an ocean, and he struggled in vain to reach the shore.

The pigeon threw a beakful of herbs into the water, and they made an island for the fly to land on. So the fly survived.

It so happened that a few moments later a poor, bare-footed tramp came by, carrying a bow and arrow. As soon as he saw the lovely plump bird he thought of his cooking pot, and in his mind he was already enjoying a feast. But just as the man prepared to kill his prey, the fly bit his heel. The man looked down to see what had hurt him. The pigeon understood what the fly was doing for her, and quick as a flash she flew away, far, far away. The soup of the poor tramp flew away with her. So because of a tiny fly, the man went pigeonless.

One day, the frogs got bored of the democratic state they lived in, and made such a fuss that Jupiter decided to send them a king. Down from the sky came a peaceful king. But he made such a mighty noise when he hit the bog that the members of the marshy tribe, all silly and full of fears, hid under the water, in the rushes, in the reeds, in holes, anywhere. For a long time they didn't even dare to peep at the face of this great giant, their king.

Now actually, their new king was a log. After some time, his silent seriousness so impressed one of the frogs that she decided to hazard a look at him. Trembling, she approached the great leader. Another frog followed, and then another, until there was a crowd. And then they started to become familiar with their king. They climbed all over him, and played jumping games on his shoulders. The good king allowed them to do what they liked, and remained quite calm.

The frogs got bored. One of them cried. 'Hey Jupiter, why don't you give us a king who can *do* something! This one's too lazy for us!'

So Jupiter sent them a new king, a crane, who gobbled up the frogs whenever he felt like it.

The frogs complained. So Jupiter said, 'What is it you want now? Do you think I'm going to change the pattern of your world every time you want something different? In the first place, you should have stuck to your own way of life, which was fine. But once you insisted on changing, you should have been satisfied to have a king who was gentle and kind. Now you can manage with what you've got. If you change again, you might get something even worse!'

aptain Fox went out one day for a walk with his friend Goat Great Horns. The goat couldn't see past the end of his nose; the fox was a past master at deception.

Soon they got thirsty and went down into a well to get some water. After they'd both had enough, the fox said, 'What shall we do now, my dear friend? Life isn't all drinking, you know. It's time we left. I'll tell you what, you raise your front hoofs high. Put them against the wall. I'll grab you by the spine, and then raise myself on your horns. That way, I can get out of the well, and then I'll pull you out after me.'

'By my beard,' replied the goat, 'that's a fine idea! It's a real pleasure to meet somebody as intelligent as you! By golly, I wish I'd thought of that!'

So, helped by the goat, the fox climbed out of the well, leaving his companion at the bottom. Then the fox leaned over and gave the goat a splendid sermon on patience. 'If Jupiter had given *you* as much sense as there is in the beard on your chin, you'd never have stepped so unthinkingly into

that well. Now, goodbye, I'm off. Try to help
yourself. Make an effort, my dear fellow! As for me,
I've important business to attend to, and must be
on my way. In any case, let me remind you of one
thing before I go: always consider the end!'

On the branch of a tree an old cock, adroit and cunning, sat on guard. Along came a fox, who said in a sugary voice, 'Brother, let us have no more quarrelling. I bear good tidings. Come down, so I can embrace you. But look, please don't keep me waiting. I have many miles to go today. In the meantime, you and yours can rest, and get on with whatever you have to do without any fear. We'll be like brothers to you. So light the fires tonight, let's have a celebration! And now, come down and let me give you a kiss of fraternal love!'

'Friend,' replied the cock, 'you couldn't say anything that would please me more than these words of peace. And to me it is a double joy to hear them from you, of all creatures. And look!.In the distance, I see two greyhounds who are without doubt rushing to bring the joyful news. One of your friends must have sent them. They are coming fast! In just a moment now they'll be with us! I'll be right down. We can all embrace one another and be friends forever.'

'Ah, farewell,' said the fox, 'I have a long journey ahead. I'll tell you what, we'll celebrate some other time, shall we?' With this, the gallant fox pulled up his breeches and ran, grief-stricken that his plan to outwit the cock had been foiled. Seeing the fox flee in terror, the old cock laughed and laughed, for it is a double pleasure to trick a trickster.

There was once a wolf who felt he wasn't catching as many sheep as he ought to, so he decided to be clever like a fox, and take on a whole new personality. He dressed up in a shepherd's costume, and made a shepherd's crook out of a bent stick. He even remembered the shepherd's pipe. If he had known how to write, he would have happily written on his hat, 'It's me, Guillot, the shepherd of this flock here!' When he was ready, he carefully laid the shepherd's crook across his front paws and sweetly approached his flock. The real Guillot was stretched out on the grass, sleeping soundly. His dog was sleeping too, and so was his pipe. Most of the sheep were asleep as well. The wolf left them asleep, but decided to persuade the others to follow him back to his fort. To do that, he figured it was necessary to imitate the shepherd's voice as well as his appearance.

Well, that ruined the whole effect. He just couldn't do it. The noise he made sounded wild, like the sort of noise you might hear in the woods, and it woke everybody up. The poor wolf got all

caught up in his shepherd's clothes and he couldn't run away or defend himself.

Imposters always give themselves away somehow. A wolf will act like a wolf. It's one of the most certain facts of life.

A certain fox, nearly dying of hunger, saw high on a trellis the most beautiful grapes in the world, juicy, ripe, all covered with a rosy skin. The gallant fox would gladly have eaten them for his lunch, but the problem was, no matter how hard he tried, he just couldn't reach them.

Finally, he said, 'They are too sour for me. They'll do for somebody who doesn't care so much about quality as I do.'

Wasn't that better than complaining about not being able to have them?

The lion, terror of the forests, full of years and mourning his lost power, was finally attacked by his own subjects, who came to see themselves as strong, now that he was weak. The horse trotted up and gave the lion a kick, the wolf bit him, the ox butted him with his horns. The miserable lion, languishing, sad and gloomy, could hardly even roar, he was so crippled by old age.

But he took all their abuse without complaint until he saw even the ass loping towards his lair. 'Ah no,' said the lion, 'It's too much. I'm willing to die, but to suffer *your* blows is to die twice over.'

It is a fact that wolves are gluttonous creatures. One wolf I heard about, who was in a merrymaking mood, ate so much so fast he nearly died. A bone got stuck in his throat, and he couldn't cry out for help. He was just about to give himself up for lost when, to his great joy, he saw a stork stalking by. He made a helpless gesture, and the stork came running. She quickly got to work and removed the bone. 'And now,' she said, 'may I have my reward?'

'Reward?' said the wolf, 'you must be joking! Isn't it enough that you've gotten your neck safely out of my throat? Get out of my sight, you ungrateful wretch! And take care never to fall under my paw.'

Miss Weasel, lovely and long and flowing and slender, wiggled into a granary through a tiny hole. She had just recovered from a long illness, so she was very thin.

She had a wonderful time in the loft, doing whatever she pleased. God knows how many little animals perished at her paws. Anyway, she got fearsomely fat and horribly heavy-jowled. At the end of the week, having eaten herself silly, she heard a noise, and decided it was time to go out through her hole.

But she couldn't get out. So she figured she must have found the wrong hole. She circled the granary a few times. Then she stopped again at her hole and said, 'I'm sure this is the place! I just don't understand! I got through here perfectly easily five or six days ago!'

A rat, seeing her all confused, took pity on her and explained: 'You were thin when you came in, miss. You've got to be thin to get out.'

This story could be told about any number of people. But let's not look too closely, or we might get them mixed up with ourselves.

The first man ever to see a camel fled at the sight. The second approached the camel. The third one made a halter for it.

Custom makes everything seem familiar. What in the beginning seems singular and terrible comes to seem ordinary in time. For example: a man is standing guard on the seacoast, and far in the distance he sees a spot. He is sure it is a powerful warship. A few moments later it becomes a freighter. Then it's a skiff, and then a bale of cotton. In the end, he sees it as a couple of sticks floating on the water.

This story would fit quite a few people. From far away, they seem to be quite something, but when they come close, they are nothing.

Let us not try to be something we are not. No matter how hard he tries, a boorish lout can't turn himself into a graceful gentleman. There are very few people who can change their personalities just because they want to — most people just have to accept themselves the way they are. Don't be like the ass in the fable who wanted his master to love him.

The poor beast said to himself, 'Why are my master and mistress so loving to their dog, and why does my master beat me all the time? Let's see. What does that dog do that I don't do? He shakes hands with his paws. Then he gets hugged and kissed. Hey, if that's all I have to do to make them care for me, that's no problem . . .'

In the midst of this happy fantasy the ass was overjoyed to see his master. He ran up to the man, raised his dirty hoof, and lovingly stroked the man's chin. And at the same time, to make himself even more adorable, he sang a gracious little song.

'Oh, oh, what a caress! What a melody!' said the master. 'Hey, boy, you with the stick! Come and beat this animal!'

The boy came running, and the donkey
changed his tune. That was the end of that comedy.

Often, great people are like actors in the theatre; their looks alone make ordinary people idolize them. But appearances are deceptive. The ass can only judge by what he sees, but the fox is more wary. He examines people, looking at them from every angle. And when he has seen through them, he describes them this way:

'They are like busts of heroes, larger than life, but hollow. It takes a lot of work to sculpt a bust. And when it's finished, it has a beautiful head, but where are the brains?' Do you know any great men who remind you of the busts of heroes?

A hare in his lair was daydreaming (what is a lair for, if not to daydream in?). He plunged himself deep into anxiety. He was a sad, sad animal. Fear gnawed at his insides.

'People who are just naturally afraid,' said he, 'are really unhappy people. They can't even digest their food. They never have a moment of pure pleasure. They always feel they're about to be attacked. Take me, for instance. I never close my eyes, even when I'm asleep. Some brainy person would probably tell me to change myself. But can fear get rid of itself? I bet lots of men are scared too, like me.'

The hare had his problem all figured out, but that didn't help him solve it. He was full of doubts, he was restless too. The merest breeze, a shadow, a nothing, would make him feverish with fear.

One day, as he was lying in the sunshine, he heard a tiny noise. This was the signal for him to flee to his hole. As he ran along he passed by the edge of a pond. Hundreds of frogs instantly jumped into the waves, rushing to get to their underwater caves.

'Hey,' said the hare. 'Don't tell me I've gone and terrified them, the way everybody does me! Wow, they really are scared of me! I've alarmed the camp! They quake before me! What do they think I am, a war hero? Oh, I see now — there's nobody in the world so cowardly that he can't find somebody who is even more scared than himself to scare.'

The ancient wizard Merlin said that those who gull others are often gulled themselves. I'm sorry to use an old-fashioned word like 'gull' but it seems to me strong. Anyway, let's get to the point.

A rat, a big, fat rat, one of the best fed of rats, who knew nothing about the higher things in life, or indeed, about much of anything besides food and drink, was playing at the edge of a bog. Along came a frog, who said in rat language, 'Ah, do come and visit my home, I'll give you a most gorgeous feast.'

The rat didn't need any convincing. 'Sure!' he said.

But the frog went on and on, telling him of the delights of bathing, the wonders and pleasures of travel, the hundred rare things the rat would see as he made his way across the swamp. 'One day,' said the frog, 'you'll be able to tell your grandchildren all about the beauties, customs and government of the underwater republic.'

Only one thing made the rat hesitate: he could swim a little bit, but he needed help. The frog had the solution to that problem. She tied her own leg to the rat's foot with a rush.

When they had swum quite far out, the gracious frog exerted all her strength to pull her guest underwater. This was against any known code of hostess honour. But then, the frog saw the rat only as a fine main course for her feast.

Already in her imagination the frog was chewing the rat to bits, while the rat was imploring the gods to come to his aid. The treacherous frog mocked him. He struggled wildly. She held on.

While they were fighting, a huge kite circled in the sky above them. The kite saw the rat beating about in the water, so he swooped down and lifted the poor drowning creature. At the same time, of course, he picked up the frog, who was tied to the rat.

Well, that was all. The bird was full of pride and joy to have caught so cleverly both meat and fish for supper.

The best laid plans can sometimes go astray, and the betrayer finds himself betrayed.

A mother goat, wanting to graze on some fresh grass and fill up her dragging teats, left the door of her house on the latch and said to her little kid, 'Promise me on your life you won't open this door to anyone, unless he whispers the password "I hate wolves" in your ear!'

Now just as she was saying this, a wolf happened to be passing by. He listened carefully to what she said, and memorized the password.

The she-goat, of course, never saw him. As soon as she was gone, the wolf made his voice all soft and murmured unctiously, 'Open the door! I hate all wolves!'

He reckoned he'd be let in straight away. But the little kid was suspicious, so he looked through the crack in the door. 'Show me your white hoof or I won't open the door!' he cried. (White hoofs are things wolves don't know much about.) The wolf was so surprised he ran all the way home. Now where would that kid be if he had put his trust in the password his mother had given him? Two precautions are worth a lot more than one. By being too careful, you never can be lost.

hat wolf reminds me of another wolf who was even better taken in. In fact, he perished. Here is the story.

A peasant lived with his family in an isolated cottage. Mr. Wolf was always hanging about near the door, watching all sorts of animals going in and out — calves and sheep and lambs, all of which he thought would make marvellous meals. But the wolf began to get tired of waiting. Then one day he heard a child cry. The mother chided the child, then scolded it, and finally yelled, 'If you don't stop all that noise I'll throw you to the wolf!'

The wolf pricked up his ears and thanked the gods for his terrific luck.

Then the mother changed her tune. 'Don't worry, don't cry my darling little one, I didn't mean it. If that big bad wolf comes near you, we'll kill him.'

'What's this?' cried the wolf, outraged. 'What do you mean by saying first one thing and then another? You think you can treat somebody like me that way? What do you take me for, an idiot? You just wait. Some day, when that beautiful little brat of yours comes to the woods to collect hazel nuts . . .'

Just as he uttered these words, out of the house rushed a dog. He grabbed the wolf, and men with spears and pitchforks came after him. 'What do you think you're doing here?' they demanded. So the wolf told them the whole story.

'What, just because of a few silly words I said, you would eat my child?' cried the mother. 'You think I've brought him up just to satisfy your hunger? You're crazy!' And they beat the poor beast to death.

Then one of the men cut off the wolf's back and front feet and took them to the mayor of the nearby village. He put up a sign on the wall of the town hall:

WOLVES:
DON'T BELIEVE EVERYTHING
A MOTHER SAYS TO HER CHILD
WHEN IT CRIES!

Horses did not always work for men. A long time ago, when human beings were still content to live off acorns picked from trees, the donkey, the horse and the mule lived in the forest. People hardly ever saw them. They had no saddles, no heavy saddle-packs, no harnesses, no carriages. They didn't have to carry men into battle, and they didn't have to take people to feasts and wedding ceremonies. In fact, there were none to go to!

Now one day, a horse had a quarrel with a stag. The stag ran away, and the horse couldn't catch him. That made the horse mad. So the horse decided to go to a man and ask for help.

The man harnessed the horse, jumped onto his back, and urged him on until they caught up with the stag. The man killed the stag.

The horse was very grateful. He said, 'Thank you. I will always remember what you did for me. Goodbye. I must now return to my life in the wild.'

'Oh no you don't,' said the man. 'You'll be much better off with us. I see very clearly that you have found your right place. You stay with me, and you'll be well treated. You'll have good food, a cosy stable, and soft hay to sleep on.'

'Alas,' said the horse, 'what good is luxury
without freedom?' The poor beast saw that he had
made a terrible mistake in asking the man for help.
But what was he to do? It was already too late. His
stable was built. He would die a slave.

He would have been much wiser to have
forgiven the stag in the first place. However
wonderful it may be to ruin somebody you hate, it
doesn't seem worth it if, to buy your triumph, you
have to give up the one thing without which
everything else is meaningless — your freedom.

'Only depend upon yourself' — that's a common saying. Here is how Aesop makes it come to life.

The larks built their nests in a field just before the wheat was ripe, that is, around the time that everyone loves, when everything in the world is growing, from ocean monsters beneath the waves to tigers in the forest and larks in the fields. But there was one lark who had let spring go halfway by without even falling in love. At last she decided to imitate nature and become a mother herself. She built a nest, laid some eggs, sat on them and made them hatch as fast as she could. It all went well. But the wheat all around the nest was ripe before her nestlings were strong enough to spread their wings and fly. The poor mother lark had a thousand different things to worry about. She had to find food for her babies, and to bring them up always to be on the lookout for danger.

One day, before she went off in search of worms, she said, 'Now look, if the owner of this field comes along with his son (and he will come), listen carefully to what he says. Depending on his words, we'll know when to leave.'

No sooner had she left than the man came along with his son. 'This wheat is ripe,' he said. 'Let's go and ask our friends to bring their sickles and help us harvest it at daybreak tomorrow.'

The mother lark returned to find her brood all alarmed. One baby bird babbled, 'He said that as soon as the sun comes up tomorrow he's coming with his friends . . .'

'If that's all he said,' replied the mother lark, 'there's no hurry for us to move. But tomorrow, listen to him carefully again. Meanwhile, be happy. Look, I've brought you some supper.' After they had eaten, they all fell asleep, the children and the mother too.

Dawn arrived, but the man's friend did not. The mother lark flew off, and the master of the field made his round as usual.

'This wheat ought not still be standing,' he told his son. 'Our friends have let us down. We were wrong to rely on such lazy people. My boy, go to our relatives and ask them to come tomorrow and help us.'

The little birds were even more terrified than they had been the day before. 'Mama,' they said, 'our hour has come, he's coming with his relatives ...'

'No, no, my little ones, sleep in peace,' said their mother. Don't budge from the nest.'

The mother lark was right, for no relatives appeared. Again the master walked around the field with his son. 'We are making a big mistake,' he said, 'in waiting for other people to help us. There is no better friend or relative than oneself. Remember that, my son. Tomorrow, we'll come to the field with our own sickles, and we'll harvest our wheat ourselves, as quickly as we can.'

When the fledglings told their mother what he had said, she said, 'It's time to go, my dears.' And they flew off, all at once, without a whisper of noise.

A peacock shed his feathers when the moulting season came. A jay picked them up and put them on. Then he paraded proudly before the other peacocks, thinking himself as beautiful as they.

The peacocks soon recognized him for what he was. They laughed at him and whistled at him, they mocked him and plucked his feathers out, so he looked very strange.

When he went home, even his friends the jays showed him the door.

There are lots of people like him, who dress themselves up in other people's old remnants. They are sometimes called copy cats, or plagiarists. But I'll be quiet. I don't want to make anybody uncomfortable. Besides, it's none of my business.

Only if you make use of what you own do you really own it. I'd like to ask those people who love to accumulate more and more wealth all the time what advantage they have over other people. It seems to me the humble man is as rich as the miser, and the proud miser lives like a beggar.

Aesop told a story about a miser who hid his treasure. This poor man was waiting to enjoy his wealth in another lifetime. He didn't possess his gold, his gold possessed him. You see, he had buried in the earth a huge sum of money, and it seemed he had buried his heart there as well, for he had no other joy in life besides ruminating day and night about that money. It was the most precious thing in the world to him; whenever he went, or whenever he came, whenever he drank or whenever he ate, there was hardly a moment that he was not brooding about the place where his fortune was buried.

Well, he went to look at the spot so often that a gravedigger saw him, and suspected that some money must be hidden there. So he dug it up, without saying a word. And one fine day, the miser found nothing but the hole.

How he cried, how he moaned, how he sighed, how he groaned. He tormented himself with anguish. A passerby asked him what the matter was.

'It's my precious treasure! Somebody has stolen my treasure!' he wept.

'Your treasure? Where was it hidden?'

'It was buried beneath this rock.'

'My goodness,' said the other man. 'Wouldn't it have been better to have kept it in your closet instead of hiding it so far from home? Then you wouldn't have had to go to so much trouble to get at it any time you needed it.'

'Any time! Good gods! Is that all you think my money was for? Does silver come as easily as it goes? I never touched it!'

'Tell me, then, if you would,' said the other man, 'why are you so upset, if you never touched your money anyway? Put a stone in its place — it will serve you just as well.'

The arts were invented a long time ago, and this story was first told in ancient Greece. But stories are worth telling again if they have meaning for the present time.

The world of the imagination is full of deserted lands. Every day, people make new discoveries there. Now this is a pretty good story. A poet named Malherbe once told it to a man named Racan. Those two could really make words sing. One day, they met each other when there was nobody else around, so they got to talking about things that worried them. Racan said, 'Tell me something please. Since you are an old man who knows all about life, you have nothing left to be afraid of. But what should I do with my life? It's about time I found out. You know me well, you can advise me. Should I move to the provinces, go into the army, become a courtier? Everything in the world seems to be a mixture of bitterness and charm. War has its sweetness, marriage its alarms. If I followed my feelings, I would know where to go. But I don't have only myself to please, I have the court and the people to think of.'

Malherbe replied, 'What, you want to please the whole world? Before I answer your question, I'll tell you a story I once read.

'An old miller and his fifteen-year-old son took their ass to sell at the fair. They wanted him to look nice and rested when he arrived, so they tied up his feet and carried him upside down, like a chandelier. They were a little bit stupid, poor things.

'The first person who saw them coming down the road started laughing. "What kind of farce is this?" he asked. "The biggest ass among the three of you isn't the one you think!"

'The miller suddenly saw how silly they were being. So he put the beast back on his feet and made him walk. The ass, who had enjoyed being carried, complained, but the miller paid no attention.

'Then the miller got his son to mount the animal while he himself walked behind. They passed three merchants. The oldest of them cried, "Hey, young man, you can't treat that old man like a lackey! Get off that donkey, and let him ride!"

' "Please, dear sirs, stop worrying," said the miller, and he and the boy quickly changed places.

'Then three girls passed by and one of them said, "Shame on you, letting that poor young man limp along, while you sit like a bishop on the donkey, making believe you are wise."

' "Don't be silly, girl," said the miller, "get on with you, I'm a tired old man." But the girls went on jeering at him, and he decided he must be wrong. So he put his son on the rump of the ass behind him.

'Then another group came along. One said, "These people are crazy. That poor ass can't stand the strain, he'll die. How dare you burden that poor animal with such a load? Have you no pity for old animals? I bet you are taking it to the fair, to sell its skin."

' "By Jove," said the miller, "I've had enough. Anybody who would try to satisfy the whole world would have to be weak in the head. Let's try and see if we can find some way to get there." So they both dismounted. The ass strutted along before them.

'Another person came along and said, "Is this the way it should be, then, the donkey going along at ease while the miller suffers? Who was made to bear burdens, the master or the ass? Look at these people! They wear out their shoes and protect their beast of burden. It's all upside down. What a bunch you are!"

'The miller replied, "I'm an ass, it's true, I agree, I confess. But from now on, whether people blame me or praise me, talk or remain silent, I'll do what I like." He did, and did well.

'As for you, my friend Racan, go to war, fall in love, become a courtier. Go, come, run, live in the country. Take a woman, be a priest or a businessman or a ruler. But make no mistake. Whatever you do, people will criticize you for it.'

Little fish grow big, assuming they remain alive at all. But still, to let one go free while you wait for it to grow up seems silly to me. It is never certain that you can catch it again.

A young carp was caught one day by a fisherman standing at the river's edge. 'Every little one counts,' said the man, when he saw his tiny catch. 'This is the beginning of a terrific feast!' And he put the fish in his bag.

The poor little carp cried out, 'Hey, what do you think you're doing? I wouldn't be more than half a mouthful for you! Please, let me grow into a big carp. Then you can catch me again! And after you've caught me, some big fat man will come along, and offer you lots of money for me. That will be better for you than if you'd found another hundred my size, which would be just enough for one meal. What kind of meal do you think I'd make? Believe me, useless.'

'You are useless, are you? Then so be it,' replied the fisherman. 'Fish, my dear friend, you make a fine preacher. In fact, you have spoken so well that tonight I'm going to put you in my frying pan. One fish in the pan is worth two in the river; one is sure, the other is not.'

One day, the iron pot suggested to the clay pot that they might take a trip together.

'I thank you kindly for inviting me,' said the clay pot, 'but I think it would be wiser for me to stay at home. It would take so little, so very little, just the tiniest thing to break me apart, and I could never be put together again. For you it's different. You've got a tough skin. Nothing can hurt you.'

'Don't worry, I'll protect you,' said the iron pot gallantly. 'If anything gets in your way I'll put myself between it and you, and save you.'

The clay pot let herself be persuaded. So they both clip-clopped along on their three feet each, as best they could. They bumped into each other every time they hit even a hiccup in the road. The clay pot suffered terribly. They had not gone a hundred paces before the iron pot had knocked his dear friend all to bits. The poor clay pot never even had a chance to complain.

If you hang around with people who are different from you, you may have the same problem as one of those pots. You may destroy another person by mistake, or get destroyed.

An old fox, still one of the best, great eater of chickens, great robber of rabbits, who could smell even another fox from a mile away, was finally caught in a trap. With great difficulty he managed to escape, but not entirely, for he left behind his tail.

Without his tail, he felt ashamed. So he decided, since he was a clever fox, to persuade the other foxes to be like him. One day, when all the foxes were at a meeting, he said, 'Hey, brothers, what are we doing with this useless weight, which sweeps all the dirty paths? What good is this long, silky tail to us? I've got an idea! Let's cut our silly old tails off! Come on, let's all join together and cut our tails off, right now.'

'That sounds like really good advice,' said one of the other foxes, 'but before we do, would you be so good as to turn around?'

At these words, all the foxes started jeering and booing so loudly that the poor tailless fox couldn't even be heard. It would have been a waste of time for him to pretend to remove his tail. The fashion continued as it was.

The most valuable thing you can do is to work well.

A rich farmer, knowing he was about to die, called his sons to his bedside. 'Whatever you do,' he said, 'never sell this land, which is our heritage. There is treasure hidden in it somewhere. I don't know where, but if you have patience, you are bound to find it some day. You must turn over the earth in your field as soon as autumn comes. Plough it up, dig deep into the earth, turn the soil over and over. Don't leave a single spot of land where your hands have not passed and passed again.'

When the father died, the sons returned to the field. They did as he had asked. They turned up the earth here, there and everywhere. They did it so well that at the end of the year it yielded a much greater crop than ever before. There was no treasure. But the father had been wise to show them before he died that work itself is a treasure.

The greedy man is likely to lose everything by trying to get everything for himself. I'll tell you just one fable to show you what I mean, the one about the hen who laid the golden eggs.

The man who owned that marvellous hen believed she had a treasure inside her body. So you know what he did? He killed her. He cut her open, and found that she was just like any other hen, physically. He had destroyed the most beautiful thing he possessed.

It would make a good lesson for stupid people, wouldn't it? How many people do you know about who become poor overnight because they want to get rich quickly?

A stag found a very high vine, the sort you see rarely, and hid behind it from some hunters and their dogs. The vine saved his life.

The hunters, you see, figured that their dogs had made a mistake when they went sniffing at that vine, so they called the dogs back.

As soon as the stag felt he was out of danger, he ate the vine. Some gratitude! The hunters heard him munching away at it, so they returned and found him.

The stag realized he was about to die, and said, 'I've earned this punishment. Profit from my example, all ungrateful wretches!'

Then the pack of hounds tore him apart. It was useless for him to complain to the hunters. This is a true picture of what happens to somebody who turns around and hurts the one who saves him.

A picture was displayed of a huge lion being vanquished by a single man. Those who saw the picture found it most glorious. A lion happened to pass by and heard the people babbling with excitement.

Said the lion, 'I can see very well that the painter has given you the victory here, man. But he has deceived you. An artist can paint anything he wants to — he's free to pretend. The lion would be the victor if my comrades knew how to paint, and with more reason.'

It's never a good idea to mock people who are sad. How can you be so sure you will always be happy yourself? Wise Aesop gives a few examples in his fables about what happens to those who laugh at others. What I'm about to say and what he says add up to the same thing.

The hare and the partridge lived together in a field, and they were happy enough, or so it seemed, until one day a hunter appeared, and the hare had to flee. He rushed to his lair, and managed to throw the dogs off his scent, but eventually he began to stink because his hole was so hot and stuffy. So the dogs found him.

One hound named Miro was a specialist in smells and he was the one who figured out that the hare was where the smell was. He chased the hare out of the lair and hurt him. Another hound, named Rustic, who never lied, announced that the hare had gone.

The poor wounded hare came back to his lair to die. The partridge said, 'Ha, ha, you're always bragging about being such a fast runner. So what did you do with your feet?'

At that moment, the partridge's turn came. She thought her wings could save her from anything. But she had forgotten all about the hawk with his cruel talons.

One day, a stag was gazing at his reflection in the clear water, admiring the beauty of his horns. But he could not look without shame at his spindly legs.

'What a terrible proportion my feet have to my head!' he said. 'My horns reach higher than all the bushes, but my legs are awful.'

Just at that moment, a bloodhound appeared. The stag leapt away through the forest to save himself. His horns kept getting tangled in the branches of the trees, so his swift feet couldn't save him. He took back everything he'd said, and cursed his lovely horns.

People always love what is beautiful, and despise what is useful. But beauty often destroys them in the end. This stag, for instance, despised his legs which made him swift. He adored his horns, and they killed him.

Two friends who were in need of money sold a bear's skin to their neighbour, the furrier. The bear was still living — but they would kill it soon, or so they said.

It was the king of all bears, they told the furrier. He would make his fortune with the skin. It would make even the coldest winter warm for whoever was fortunate enough to wear it. In fact, it would make two coats, not just one.

The famous sheep-stealer Dindenaut was less proud of his sheep than they were of their bear. (The bear was theirs by *their* reckoning, but not by the bear's.)

The two men offered to deliver the skin in two days at the very outside. So they agreed a price. Then they set out to find the bear. They found him all right, coming towards them at a fast trot. What could they do? They didn't stop to settle terms with the bear. One of the men climbed a tree. The other, colder than marble with fear, lay down on his tummy, held his breath, and played dead. (He had heard somewhere that bears rarely eat a corpse.)

The bear, like a fool, fell for this ploy. He saw the body lying there, and figured the man was dead. But he thought it might be a trick, so he turned the man over, leaned over his nostrils, and smelled his breath.

Then he announced, 'It's a corpse all right. It stinks. I'm getting out of here.' And away he ran into the forest.

The other man climbed down from his hiding place. 'Wow,' he said, 'it's a wonder we were only scared, and not killed! I see you didn't get the skin, ha, ha! But tell me, what did the bear whisper in your ear? He certainly got close enough!'

The man lying on the ground replied primly, 'He told me never to sell the skin of a bear until the bear has finished with it.'

One day, an ass dressed up in a lion's skin and went about scaring everybody for miles around. He was as weak as could be, but he made the world tremble.

Then came the moment when the tip of his ear stuck out, and showed him for what he really was. When he saw the donkey's ear, the donkey boy set to work on him. The gullible townspeople were amazed when they saw the boy chasing the lion to the mill.

There are plenty of people like that donkey, who act important. Three quarters of their worth is in the trappings they surround themselves with.

A baby mouse who had no experience of life was nearly caught. This is how he told the story to his mother:

'I leapt across the mountains bordering this country, and dashed along like a young rat, seeking to know the world. Suddenly, two animals caught my eye. One of them was sweet, kind and gracious. The other was wild and noisy. He had a piercing shriek. His head was topped by a hideous piece of flesh. And he raised his strange arms just as though he was planning to fly away. His tail was all spread out in plumes.'

Now this animal, which the mouse described so vividly as though it were a beast from the wilds of America, was in fact a cock.

'He hit his arms against his flanks,' the mouse went on, 'making such an uproar, that even I, who pride myself on my courage, took flight in terror, though I bravely shouted nasty things to him as I ran. If it hadn't been for that monster, I'd have been able to make friends with the other animal, who seemed lovely. He was a velvety creature, like us, and spotted. He had a long tail, and a modest

look. Yet his eyes were so shining! I think he's a very sympathetic type, mama, to the mouse family, at least. Even his ears are shaped somewhat like ours. I was just about to go up to him and make friends when, with a thunderous noise, the other one made me flee.'

'My son,' said his mother, 'this sweet creature you are so delighted with is a cat. Under his false smile hides our greatest enemy. The other animal, the noisy one, is far from doing us harm. In fact, he will some day be the main course at our dinner table. As for the cat, his cuisine is largely based on us. So watch out. As long as you live, don't judge by appearances.'

The Dog who Let Go of His Prey
for its Reflection

People are always deceiving themselves. You
see so many crazy people running after shadows, it
would be impossible to count them. Aesop tells of
a dog who caught a small animal near the edge of
a stream. When he leaned over the water, he saw
the little animal reflected in the water, and dropped
it so he could catch its image. The dog fell into the
stream and nearly drowned. He managed to get
himself safely back onto the bank, but he had lost
both the shadow and the substance of his prey.

A mule belonging to a priest prided himself on his nobility. He talked endlessly about his elegant mother, the mare — how she had done such and such a thing, and been to such and such a place. The mule reckoned that the fact that he had such a special mother was a good enough reason for *him* to be famous.

After some time, he became the servant of a doctor, and that made him feel all sad and humiliated.

When he was old, he had to go to work for a miller. Finally, he remembered that he had had a father as well as a mother, and that his father had been a mere donkey.

If suffering does no more than bring a fool to his senses, that's enough.

In the Middle East there is a legend about
a certain rat who got tired of the world and all its
cares and retired into an Edam cheese. The silence
there was deep, and filled his whole round cheese of
a world. The rat wasn't used to being a hermit, but
he managed somehow to stay alive. In fact, he dug
about so much with his feet and teeth that in a few
days he had made, at the bottom of his cheese,
a room to live in and plenty of food to live on. What
more could he want? He became sleek and fat. It
seemed that God protected those who devoted their
lives to Him.

Well, one day some representatives of the rat
population came to this religious rat, to beg him for
help in their war against the cat. They had been
forced to flee their country for a strange land. Rat
City was blocked off, and they hadn't been able to
take any money with them when they fled. They
didn't need much, just enough to tide them over
until help would arrive, in less than a week.

'My dear friends,' said the hermit rat, 'wordly
things are no longer of any interest to me. In what
way could a poor recluse like myself possibly assist

you? What can I do, except pray to God, and ask Him to help you? I sincerely hope He does.'

So saying, he slammed the door in their faces. Now who do you suppose I'm talking about? Was this rat a monk? No, surely a heathen. Monks are always kind, or so I suppose.

esop tells the story of a peasant, more kind than wise, who was strolling around his fields one day when he saw a snake stretched out on the snow, frozen stiff. It was clear the snake wouldn't live more than a few minutes more if he were left there. So the man took him in his arms and carried him home and laid him along the hearth and brought him back to life. The man never considered what his reward might be for this kind act.

Well, for a while the poor numb beast scarcely felt a thing, but gradually his spirit revived, and with it his anger. He raised his head, hissed, coiled his body and tried to strike his rescuer.

'Ungrateful wretch!' shouted the peasant. 'Is this the way you pay me for saving your life? Then die!' And he seized his axe and struck the snake twice, making three serpents in two blows — head, trunk and tail. The pieces flapped about trying to come together again, but they couldn't.

It's good to be kind — but to whom? That is an important question. And as for ungrateful cads, they are bound to die miserable deaths.

It is important for people to help one another. For instance, supposing your neighbour has just died — you are the one who has to bear the burden.

A donkey and a horse were going down the road together. The horse was carrying nothing but his own harness, but the poor donkey was so heavily loaded he could barely stagger along at all.

'Please,' said the donkey, 'won't you help me? Otherwise I shall die before we reach town.' He paused. No answer.

'It's not unreasonable, what I ask,' he continued. 'If you took half of this burden, it would be no more than a toy for you, so we'd both be happy.'

The horse refused, and gave a loud fart.

Then the donkey did die, and the horse realized he'd made a grave mistake. He had to carry not only the donkey's whole load, but the donkey's carcass, on top of that.

A farmer with a cartful of hay got stuck in a mire, far from all human help, near some village in Brittany called Quimper-Corentin. It often happens that if Fate is angry at somebody he sends him to that spot! I hope I never end up there.

Anyway, to get back to the farmer stuck in the mud. There he was, cursing and carrying on generally, yelling about the holes in the road, yelling about his horrible horses, blaming his stupid cart, swearing at himself. Finally, he called out to the god who is famous for his strength.

'Hercules,' he cried, 'please help me! If you were able to carry this whole world on your back once, surely you are strong enough to get me out of this mud now!'

A voice from the sky answered him. 'Hercules likes people who bestir themselves — those are the kind he helps. You've got to look for the source of your problem. First, get all that mud and mortar away from the wheels. All right? Now, take your pick, and break the obstacle that's in your way. Then fill up the ruts. Have you done all that?'

'Yes,' said the man after some time.

'Now before I help you,' said the voice, 'take hold of your whip.'

'I've got it,' said the man in an exhausted little voice. 'Hey, what's this? My cart is going beautifully! Praise be to Hercules!'

Then he heard the voice again. 'You see how easily your horses got out of that mire? If you first help yourself, then the gods will help you.'

The king of the animals was lying sick in his den. He sent a messenger out to tell all his subjects that a representative of every type of animal was to come and visit him. For his part, he promised in writing that they would come to no harm; he would not tear them apart with his teeth or his claws.

So all the different groups of animals sent along their deputies — all, that is, except the foxes. The foxes stayed at home, for, as one of them pointed out, the footprints of all those animals who had gone to pay their respects to the lion went up to the entrance of the lion's den, but none of them came back again.

That worried the foxes. So they thanked the lion's messenger kindly for the invitation, but declined it.

A sickness filled the whole world with terror — the plague. It looked as though the plague would keep the ferrymen busy for a long time carrying the souls of the dead across the River Acheron to hell.

It was a disease which made war on all the animals. They didn't all die, but they all lost their will to live. No longer did the wolf and fox lie in wait for their sweet and innocent prey. Doves fled; no more love, no more joy.

The lion called a meeting and said, 'My dear friends, I believe God has sent this plague to punish us for our sins. If the guiltiest one of us were willing to sacrifice himself for the sake of the others, maybe he could gain salvation for the rest. History has shown us that martyrs can redeem the world. So let's not be kind to ourselves. Let us look without self-indulgence at the state of our conscience. I, for instance, have to admit that to satisfy my greed I have devoured an awful lot of sheep. Yet what did they ever do to me? No harm. In fact, I sometimes even ate the shepherd. So I will gladly sacrifice myself if necessary. But I think it would be a good idea if you all examined your soul as I have done.

That way, we can hope that justice will be done, and that only the worst one will perish.'

'Sir,' said the fox, 'you are far too good a king. Your scruples show too much delicacy. What, you think eating sheep, rabble like that, is a crime? No, no, you do them an honour to crack their bones in your jaws. And as for the shepherd — well, you could say he got what he deserved. People have based their whole lives on destroying animals.'

All the other animals cheered the fox's words. No one wanted to examine too closely the tiny offences of the tiger, the bear, or the other important members of the animal kingdom. All of them, even to the wild dog, seemed to be saints.

When it was the ass's turn to speak he said, 'I remember once, I was passing by the meadow of some monks. Hunger, chance (the monks were away that morning), the tenderness of the grass, and, I suppose some devil, prompted me to graze in that field until I was full. I had no right, and that's the truth.'

As soon as he finished speaking, the other animals yelled, 'Shame, shame! That's horrible!'

Then a rather clever wolf made a rather complicated speech which proved that it was necessary for them to sacrifice the wicked ass, who was a bald and scabby monster, and the cause of all their problems. The ass's little sin was judged a case for hanging. To eat people's grass! What an awful thing to do! He deserved to die.

From this story you can see that depending on whether you are powerful or weak you will be judged good or bad.

P errette was walking along with a pot of milk balanced nicely on a cushion on her head. She was imagining how it would be when she got to the market. She had dressed simply so she could move easily, and she wore flat shoes so she could take big steps and get to town quickly. She was already counting and spending, in her mind, the money she would get for the milk. She bought a hundred imaginary eggs, and they hatched into three hundred imaginary chickens. They grew up strong and healthy, thanks to her care.

'Why it's easy,' she said to herself, 'for me to raise chickens. The fox will have to be very clever not to leave me enough of them to trade in for a pig. The pig will already be quite big when I get him, and to make him fat, I'll only need a little grain. Then I'll exchange him for money, and with that money I'll buy a cow and her calf to fill the stable. I can see them now, frolicking about with the sheep . . .'

At that point in her daydream, Perrette got so excited that she took a frolicking little leap herself, and the milk pot fell off her head. Goodbye calf, goodbye cow, goodbye pig and brood of chicks. The owner of all these fantastic animals sadly left her lost fortune spilt on the road, and went home to tell her husband, and probably to get beaten by him.

This sad story is now ended. I'll call it 'The Pot of Milk'. Who doesn't build castles in Spain? Kings, milkmaids, wisemen, fools — everyone does.

Everyone daydreams — there is nothing more fun to do. We get carried away in the bliss of self deception, and all that is good in the world seems to be meant just for us, all the honours, all the lovely women, whatever. When I'm by myself I can defy the bravest man in the world. My mind rambles. I dethrone the Shah. The people ask me to take his place. They love me. Diadems are showered upon my head. But if by some accident I'm brought back to myself, I'm just fat John, as I always was.

J ust being able to run isn't enough; you have to start on time. Here is an example of what I mean.

One day, the tortoise said to the hare, 'I'll bet you can't beat me in a race.'

'You've got to be joking,' said the hare. 'You must be crazy. My dear girl, maybe you should go purge yourself with about four grains of hellebore, a well-known remedy for insanity.'

'Crazy or not,' said the tortoise, 'I bet you can't beat me.'

So they agreed to have a race, and each of them placed a stake at the goal. I don't know how much they bet, or who the umpire was, but that's not important.

The hare had only to take four leaps — I mean the kind of leaps he would take if dogs were after him, when he could move so fast they'd be running till doomsday to catch up, forever measuring the landscape behind him. So he knew he had plenty of time to rest, to graze, to sleep, to listen to which way the wind blew, while he let the tortoise puff along like a senator.

The tortoise went as fast as she could, she made haste slowly. Meanwhile, the hare, scorning an easy victory, believed it would look a lot better if he started late. He ate, he rested, he fooled around, he even forgot about the bet. Finally, when he saw that the tortoise had nearly reached the end of the race course, he flew like an arrow. But his effort was in vain. The tortoise arrived first.

'So,' cried the tortoise, 'who was right? What good is your speed? I won the race! I wonder where *you'd* be if you carried a house on your back?'

Is there anyone who doesn't chase after Fortune? I'd love to be able to sit back and watch everybody endlessly rushing from kingdom to kingdom, trying to find destiny's lovely daughter, all faithfully pursuing a fickle illusion. For just as they are about to embrace her, the inconstant woman slips out of reach. Poor men! I feel sorry for them. One must have more pity than anger for fools.

I hear them saying things like, 'Just look at that man! He used to plant cabbages, and now he's pope! Aren't we as good as he is?'

And I say quietly, so they can't hear me, 'You are better! But what good is merit? Has Fortune eyes to see? And then, what about being pope, anyway? Do you really think its worth giving up your leisure for? Leisure is a treasure so precious that it once belonged only to the gods. Fortune doesn't often give it to the men she stays with. Don't chase after her. Let her chase you — women are used to it.'

There were two men who lived in a nice little village. One of them spent his time pining after Fortune. One day, he said to his friend, 'Hey, why don't we leave this place? No man is a prophet in his own country: let's seek our luck somewhere else.'

'You go,' replied his friend. 'I don't want a better climate or a happier life. You do what you like — follow your restless mind. You'll be back! I think I'll just go to sleep till you return.'

The ambitious one, or the greedy one (depending on your point of view) went down many roads and paths. He arrived the next day at a place where the exotic goddess was known to spend a lot of time — the court. There he stayed for quite a while. He did everything that everybody else did, in the right way, at the right time. But where he expected everything, he got nothing.

'What's this?' he said, 'I'll look somewhere else. I know Fortune still lives here, I see her every day, going in and out of people's houses. So why doesn't she ever come and visit me? I guess they were right when they told me that ambitious men are not much liked around here. So goodbye, courtiers. You can go on chasing shadows: I'm getting out of here. They say that Fortune has some fine temples at Surat.' And off he went.

If it's true, as they say, that human beings have spirits of bronze, his must have been plated with diamonds; for to attempt that journey was madness. Often during the voyage he longed for his village. He was attacked by pirates, by winds, halted on

a sea of utter calm, battered by rocks. He suffered terribly, seeking his death in faraway lands. Even death could have found him just as easily if he had stayed at home.

Finally, the man arrived in India. There he was told that Fortune had just gone to Japan. He rushed off to Japan. The sea was lazy, loath to take him there. And all he got from the long voyage was the lesson the savages taught him: live in your own country, as nature wants you to.

At last, he admitted he'd made a terrible mistake. He gave up his plan and returned to his own country. When he saw his house from a distance, he cried with joy, and said, 'Happy the man who lives at home, making the best of what he's got. He has only *heard* about the court, the sea, the distant empires, and Fortune, who tempts us to the edge of the world, waving in front of our eyes her fame and wealth, without ever keeping her promises. From now on, I'm never leaving my own house. I'll be a hundred times happier.'

As he was resolving never to have anything to do with Fortune again, he looked up and saw her sitting at the door of his old friend's house. His friend was inside, fast asleep.

One day, the heron, going who knows where on his long legs, with his long beak stuck out and his long neck craning, wandered along by the side of a river. The water was transparent, as it is on perfect days.

A carp was going round and round in circles in the water with her friend the pike. The heron could easily have caught them both. They were so close to the surface, he had only to reach out and take them. But he thought it would be better to wait until lunchtime (he only ate at certain hours, he liked routine).

After some moments, it occurred to him that lunchtime had arrived. He saw some little fish, tench, who had swum up from the bottom. 'I don't want those old tench,' he said, 'I'm a heron, I don't eat tench! Who do they think I am, that I should eat tench?'

Then he saw a gudgeon. 'Gudgeon! What kind of a meal is that for a heron? I should open my beak for so little? The gods would not approve!'

As it happened, he was to open his beak for much less. He saw no more fish. Hunger seized

him, and he was thrilled when he came upon
a snail.

   Those who are easy to please are the most
intelligent. If you try to get too much, you risk
losing everything. It's better not to despise
anything, especially if it's close to being just what
you need.

His majesty the lion decided one day to find out how many nations he was master of. He sent his deputies to every corner of the forest with a gracious invitation, bearing his seal, which said that for the next month the king would be holding court. First there would be a huge feast, followed by monkeys doing fancy tricks.

This was his way of showing his subjects how powerful he was, and how grand. He invited them into his palace. What a palace! It was a real charnel house. The smell was terrible.

The bear held his nose, which was not a clever thing to do. The lion wasn't pleased, and immediately killed him, to teach him a lesson. The monkey thought that was marvellous. He fawned on the lion, praising him for his monstrous temper, for his magnificent claws, for his elegant palace, and above all for the smell.

'There is no perfume, no flower, which would not smell like garlic compared to this heavenly odour.' But his crazy flattery was not a success, and he was punished the same way the bear had been. The lion was quite a nasty sort.

The fox was standing nearby. 'Ha!' said the lion, 'tell me, Mr. Fox, what do *you* think of the smell here? Be frank with me!'

'I'b awfully sorry,' said the fox, 'I hab a bad cold so I ca't smell anythig.'

It seems that if you want to please people at court, it's best not be honest, like the bear, but not to be a flatterer either. And try, whenever possible, to avoid answering questions.

One fine morning, Mrs. Weasel took over the house of a young rabbit. She was sly. The rabbit was out, so it was an easy thing to do. She carried all her goods and chattels to her new home, while the rabbit paid court to the sun, and played in the dew-covered thyme. When he had grazed and run about till he was tired, little John rabbit returned to his home in the ground. The weasel was watching from the window.

'Oh protecting gods, what's happening?' cried the poor little rabbit. 'I've been ousted from my family estate! Listen, Mrs. Weasel, you get out of here, or I'll call all the rats in the country to chase you out.'

The lady with the pointed nose replied that the land belonged to the first inhabitant. That was a terrific defence, since she had sneaked in while the owner was gone. 'And when this place becomes a kingdom,' she said, 'I'd like to know what law is going to say that John, son of Peter or William should inherit the place, rather than Paul or me.'

Little John reminded her of the rights that come with custom and usage. 'This place has been

handed down from father to son to son,' he said.
'For you to have a right to it just because you got
here before me — would that be more just?'

'Let's not fight about these petty issues,' said
the weasel. 'Let's take the case to Raminagrobis and
let him decide.'

Now Raminagrobis was a slick, sleek,
smooth-talking cat who lived alone. 'A hermit,' said
the weasel, 'a saint of a cat, furry and fat. He's an
expert in this kind of thing.'

John rabbit agreed, and the two of them went
to visit the cat. Raminagrobis said, 'My dear
children, approach. I am deaf, old age has caught up
with me.'

They both drew closer to the cat, fearing
nothing. As soon as they got close enough,
Raminagrobis made peace between them at once,
by eating them together.

This is a little bit like the situation you see sometimes when landlords who are fighting with each other take their problem to the king.

Along a mountain path, steep and sandy, exposed to the burning sun, six strong horses were pulling a heavy coach. All the people had got out of the coach, even the women, the old people and a monk. The horses were staggering with exhaustion.

Then along came a fly, and started bothering the horses. First she tried to arouse them with her buzzing. Then she pricked them, one after another, and thought *she* was making them go. She perched on the cart pole, on the nose of the driver, and whenever the cart went forward, she thought *she* made it go.

She acted like a leader in a battle, rushing around everywhere, making the troops advance, egging them on to victory. In this common cause, the fly kept complaining that she was the only one who was doing anything, that nobody else would share the responsibility. The monk was saying his prayers. He was taking his time! A woman was singing. What did she have to sing about? The fly herself would be happy to sing in their ears, if that was what was required!

And she did just that, and a hundred other foolish things as well. After a long time and a lot of work, the coach arrived at the top.

'We will stop and rest now,' said the fly. 'I've gotten you all to the top. Please pay me for my pains.'

That's the way some people are. They throw their weight around, and interfere in everybody's business. They see themselves as indspensable. They should be chased away.

It is a fact that what God does, he does well.
Without having to look for proof throughout the
universe, I find it in pumpkins.

A peasant was once reflecting on pumpkins,
on how odd it was that the pumpkin is so huge, and
its stalk is so thin.

'What possessed God,' he wondered, 'to make
it such a way. He has really misplaced the pumpkin!
By God, if I'd been God, I'd have hung it from one
of those mighty oaks! That would be appropriate.
Such a fruit, such a tree, how beautifully they'd go
together. It's a pity that I wasn't there to advise God
when He made the world. Everything would have
been so much better. For instance, why didn't He
put the acorn, which isn't even as big as my little
finger, on the pumpkin's slender stalk? Now that
would have made sense. Poor God was confused.
The more I contemplate these plants, the more it
seems to me that He has made a terrible blunder.'

These thoughts perplexed the man. 'One can't
even sleep,' he said, 'when one is as brilliant as me.'
So saying, he lay down under an oak tree to take
a nap. An acorn fell and hurt his nose. He woke up,

and feeling his face, he found the acorn caught in his beard.

His injured nose made him change his tune. 'Hey, I'm bleeding!' he cried. 'And what if it had been a pumpkin that fell on my nose, instead of this acorn? God didn't want that to happen. Without doubt, He was right. Now I understand God very well.' And praising God for everything He'd done, the man returned home.

decrepit, gouty old lion decided it was time to find a remedy for old age. 'Nothing is impossible for a king,' he said, 'the very idea that it might be is an insult.' So he sent word to all the doctors from all over the place, asking them to bring in their solutions for the problems of old age.

The fox doctor excused himself, and stayed quietly at home. The wolf doctor paid his respects to the king, and made snide remarks about his absent friend. So the king instantly decided the fox should be smoked out of his den and made to come.

The fox came, and was presented to the king. Knowing the wolf had been saying nasty things about him, he said, 'I fear, your majesty, that you have heard some false report concerning my absence from your side. In fact, I was on a pilgrimage. I was offering up prayers for your health. And on my journey, I met some experts. I told them of the terrible weakness which so worries your majesty, and they said all you need is heat. What you need to do is skin a wolf alive, and apply his skin, all hot and smoking, to yours. This is the remedy for when your natural functions fail. Perhaps, if you wish, Mr. Wolf will serve as your dressing gown.'

The lion thought this a marvellous idea. He had the wolf skinned and dismembered. Then he ate the flesh and wrapped himself in the skin.

So, people of the court, it's better not to be nasty about one another. Try to pay homage to the king without slandering people. If you say things against other people, they'll do four times as much harm to you. You are in a career where nothing is ever forgiven.

A cobbler sang from morning to night, of marvels he'd seen and heard. He travelled through life more happy than the seven sages of ancient Greece. His neighbour, on the other hand, was rolling in money, but he sang little and slept even less. He was an important man in the business world.

Every time the financier decided to take a nap, the cobbler's singing kept him awake. The rich man complained that all the money in the world could not buy sleep, the way it bought food and drink. So one day, he invited his cheerful neighbour over to his house, and said, 'Now tell me, how much do you earn in a year, hm?'

'In a year? My goodness, mister, it's not my style to count that way,' said the cobbler, laughing. 'I earn almost nothing from one day to the next. I'm happy if I get to the end of the year! Each day brings its bread.'

'All right, all right, how much do you make in a day then?' asked the businessman impatiently.

'Sometimes more, sometimes less. I have only one problem — my work keeps getting interrupted by holidays. Each one is more of a bore than the last, since I can't work. And the parson is always finding new saints to celebrate.'

The financier laughed at the cobbler's simplicity, and said, 'I'll tell you what, I'll set you up

like a lord. Take this hundred crowns. Guard them carefully, so you'll have them when you need them.'

To the cobbler, a hundred crowns was like all the silver that had been produced for the use of all the men in the world for the last hundred years. He returned home. In his cellar, he buried his money. Sleep left his home, he had for friends nothing but worries, suspicions and vain alarms. All day he looked out for thieves; at night, if a cat moved, the cat was stealing his money.

In the end, he ran to the house of the man he no longer kept awake. 'Give me my songs and my sleep,' he said, 'and please take your hundred crowns!'

Our eyes are never safe from beauty, nor can we draw our hands away from gold. There are not very many people who will guard another's treasure faithfully.

There was once a dog, who always carried his master's dinner around his neck. He had learned to be very restrained, more restrained than he liked to be.

One day, he was given a marvellous morsel to carry. He wanted so badly to eat it, but he didn't. I wonder how many people would be so good! It's funny, you can teach dogs to be self-sacrificing, but you can't teach people. Anyway, this dog was loping along when he met a mastiff who tried to take the food. It wasn't as easy as the mastiff expected. The dog put the food down and fought with him. It was quite a fight. Then some other dogs arrived, street dogs who weren't afraid of anything. The first dog saw that he was outnumbered, and that the meat was going to get eaten. So he grabbed what he could. 'A small piece will do me, you guys have the rest!' he said. Then they all pulled the rest apart. Everyone got some.

This story reminds me of a town in which only scraps are left for the ordinary people. The important people take everything they can. The cleverest one sets the example. It's quite a pastime to watch them clear out the money from the coffers.

Sometimes, one who is in a position of power might try to defend the public money, so the people who deserve it can get it. He is called an idiot by the other important people. So it doesn't cause him a lot of pain to give up his ideals. In fact, he's often the first to dig into the cash.

A not very bright rat lived in a field. One day he got restless, and decided it was time to see the world. So he left the field, the golden grain, the sheaves of corn, and as soon as he got past the boundaries, he said, 'Wow, what a world! Hey look, there are the Apennines, and there are the Caucasian Mountains!' He saw the least little mound as a mountain.

After some days, he arrived at the shore where the tide had left loads of oysters. 'The high seas!' he said. 'And look at all those ships! My poor old dad never dared to travel, he was scared of everything. Now me, I've seen the maritime empire; I've passed through deserts, and gone thirsty.'

Just in one tiny village the rat picked up all these ideas, and he talked about them whenever he could. He wasn't one of those rats who have to chew up books to make themselves wise.

Now among all those closed oysters was one open oyster, gaping at the sun, enjoying the breeze, breathing in and expanding, all white and fat, unbeatably delicious to look at. The rat saw it from quite far away. 'What have we here!' he cried. 'It is food! And unless I am much mistaken, if I don't eat it today, I never will.'

So master rat, full of happy hope, approached the oyster, stretched out his neck and bit — and found himself caught in a trap. In an instant, the oyster had closed up. So much for ignorance.

This fable contains more than one lesson. First — those who know least about the world are astonished by any old thing. And second — whoever tries to take somebody in gets taken in himself.

There was a certain mountain bear who had been confined by fate to a solitary life in the woods. Living hidden and alone, he had become quite crazy. It's good to talk, and better to be quiet — but either one is bad when carried too far. No other animal lived within miles of the bear. The poor thing became very sad, very depressed.

Now not far away lived an old man, who had much the same problem as the bear. He loved his garden, and tended it well, he grew beautiful flowers and wonderful fruits. He was happy doing that, but sometimes he wanted to talk to someone, since plants don't talk much.

So one day, this old man went out to see if he could find himself a friend. The bear happened to leave his den the same day, also looking for a friend. They came upon each other at a turning in the path.

The man was afraid. But what could he do? It seemed best to hide his fear. The bear, who wasn't very smooth socially, growled, 'Come and visit me!'

The old man replied, 'Sir, you can see my house from here. If you would do me the honour of being my guest for a simple repast, I've got some fruit and milk. It is not, perhaps, what bears are used to, but I offer what I have.'

The bear gladly accepted, and off they went together. Before they got to the house they were already good friends; by the time they arrived, they were wonderful friends. And although it might seem to you that it is better to be alone than to be with somebody stupid, as the bear never spoke two words in a day, the man was able to devote himself to his work. The bear went hunting, and brought back game. He made it his main job to protect his friend from flies, and every night, he whisked them away from the old man's face as he slept.

One night, when the man was fast asleep, a fly landed on the tip of his nose. The bear was in despair. 'I must get that fly!' he exclaimed. No sooner said than done; the faithful flycatcher seized a stone and threw it hard. It killed the fly all right, but it killed the man too. The bear was as good a thrower as he was a bad reasoner, and his friend was stiff and dead on the bed.

Nothing is as dangerous as a stupid friend. It is better to have a wise enemy.

The lion's wife died.

Right away, all the animals rushed to tell the king of beasts how sorry they were.

The lion announced that the funeral would be held at a certain time, at a certain place. As you can guess, everyone came. The king abandoned himself to grief, and his den rocked with the noise (lions have no other church but their own home to hold funerals in). Everyone followed his example, each animal roaring in his own language. (My definition of a court is a place where all do whatever pleases the prince, whether they want to or not. If they can't be as he wishes, they at least try to look the way he wants them to. They are chameleons, who change colour at his whim; they are monkeys, who dance to his music; it's as though one mind is in charge of a thousand bodies; courtiers are simple in their motives.)

Anyway, to get back to my story. The stag didn't cry. How could he? This death was sweet to him. The lion queen had strangled both his wife and son. So he didn't cry.

One of the flatterers told the king that he had seen the stag laughing. The anger of a king is terrible, as wise King Solomon once said, and especially the anger of a lion king. But the stag hadn't read what King Solomon said — he didn't read much. Anyway, King Lion said to him, 'You low creature, how dare you laugh? You are not worthy to be punished by my sacred claws. Come wolves, revenge my queen. Tear this traitor apart!'

Then the stag said, 'Sire, the time for tears is past. Sadness is no longer the point. Your wonderful wife, sleeping among the flowers, appeared to me in a vision. I recognized her at once. "Friend," she said to me, "take care not to weep at my funeral. In heaven, I have already tasted a thousand charms, talking to those who are saints like myself. But let my husband grieve at my death for a while; that will make me happy."'

The stag had scarcely finished speaking when all the animals began to cry, 'Miracle! The queen has risen!'

So the stag was rewarded, not punished.

Amuse kings with dreams, flatter them, tell them lies to make them happy. Then, however angry they may have been before, they'll love you.

Ever since goats first began to graze, they've had the kind of independent natures that makes them chase after fortune. They go to the places that others stay away from; they are happiest playing in a place with no tracks or paths nearby. And nothing can stop them from climbing.

Two goats, both fancy-free, elegant on their white feet, left the lower pasture separately. By chance they met. They came to a brook which had a plank across it for a bridge.

Two little weasels could have just about gotten past each other on that bridge. And the rapid current would have made even them tremble. Despite the danger, one of the goats set foot on the plank, so the other did too. They acted like two kings approaching each other, neither wanting to be first (or last). Each advanced, step by step, until they were nose to nose. Each saw himself as very special, and when they came to the middle, neither would make way for the other.

You see, each of them had wonderful ancestors which made him believe he was better than the other. So, since neither one would give way, they both fell into the rushing torrent. This kind of accident is nothing new in the world.

It's one of nature's laws that we should help one another. The ass, however, forgot this one day. I don't know why, since he was usually a nice ass. He and his friend the dog were taken to the country by their master. They walked along quietly behind the man, until he fell asleep, and then the ass began to graze. They were in a meadow full of the most wonderful green grass. The dog was dying of hunger, and he didn't like grass. He said to his friend, 'Dear donkey, please bend down so I can get at the bread-basket you are carrying.'

The ass was too busy eating to answer. He was so afraid he might lose a bite of grass, he pretended not to hear. The dog went on begging, and finally the ass said, 'My dear dog, let me give you some good advice. Wait until our master wakes up and he'll feed you. Be patient. It won't be long.'

Just then, a wolf came bounding towards them from the woods. He, too, was hungry. The donkey said to the dog, 'Help me, help me!'

The dog didn't budge. He said, 'My dear ass, let me give you some good advice. Why don't you flee until our master wakes up? It won't be long, and he

is sure to help you. In the mean time, if the wolf catches you, kick him in the jaw. You're wearing nice new shoes. I'm sure you'll knock him out.'

While he was talking, the wolf strangled the ass. I conclude it's better if we help one another.

The cat and the fox, like beautiful saints, went on a pilgrimage together. They were really just pretending to be religious, and they ate lots of chickens and cheeses along the way, to pay themselves back for all their expenses.

The journey was long, and they got bored. To make the time pass more quickly, they fought. That was a great help. Otherwise, they would have slept the whole time. They made themselves hoarse with quarrelling. When they had finally exhausted all their arguments, they talked about their plans for the next day.

After a while, the fox said to the cat, 'You act clever. But do you think you know as much as me? I have a hundred tricks in my sack.'

'I don't think I know as much as you,' said the cat. 'I have only one trick. But I bet it's worth a thousand of yours.'

So they were fighting again, this time about who was cleverest.

A pack of hounds interrupted them. The cat said to the fox, 'Now search in your sack my friend. Or find in that cunning brain of yours a way to escape. As for me, here's my method.' And he jumped into a tree.

The fox circled the tree, round and round. Then he crept into a hundred holes, and came out again. None of them was good enough. The hunters smoked him out of one, at last, and set their hounds on him as he tried flying through the air. They killed him.

It's not a good idea to have too many tricks up your sleeve, or in your sack, or in your head. You waste an awful lot of time deciding which one to use. It's better to have one good trick.

O nce upon a time there was a giddy tortoise who, weary of her hole, decided to see the world. Those who have never travelled believe faraway lands are the best; those who can hardly move are quick to hate their houses.

So the tortoise made friends with a couple of ducks, and told them her plans. They said they'd be glad to help her.

'See this huge path we fly along? We're going by air to America! When you get there, you'll see everything — republics, kingdoms, all different kinds of people, and you'll learn about their customs. You'll be just like the wandering hero Ulysses.'

The tortoise wasn't particularly interested in being like Ulysses. But she was very interested in travel, and she loved their idea. So the ducks worked out a way to carry her. They held a stick between their beaks and said, 'Now, hold this tight in your mouth and don't let go!' Then they lifted the stick with the tortoise into the air. Everyone down below them was amazed when they saw the slow old tortoise flying through the air with her house on her back, along with two birds.

'It's a miracle!' they cried. 'Come and look! The queen of tortoises is flying through the clouds!'

'The queen of tortoises, that's right. That's who I am all right! Now I guess you won't laugh at me any more!' shouted the tortoise triumphantly.

She would have been better off if she'd said nothing. As soon as she let go of the stick she crashed to the ground and split open at the feet of those who had been shouting her praises. She was killed, just because she couldn't keep from boasting. Silly babbling, curiosity and vanity are all members of the same family.

There wasn't a pond in all the area that didn't contribute little fish to that great bird, the cormorant. All the pools of water, even the tiniest, supplied his needs. He ate very well; but when old age glazed him, he couldn't catch so many fish as before.

Every cormorant has to provide for himself. This one, a little too old to see beneath the surface of the water, and not having any nets, began to really suffer from lack of food. What was he to do? Need, the teacher of technique, gave him a bright idea. On the edge of one pond, the cormorant saw a crab.

'My friend,' said the bird, 'come here a minute. I have something to say to you. It looks to me like you and your folks are all about to die. The owner of this place is going fishing in eight days.'

The crab rushed to tell all the fish. They were in a frenzy. They sent a representative to the cormorant. 'Sir,' said he, 'where did you hear this terrible news? Are you sure? Do you know anything we can do?'

'Move,' said the cormorant.

The Fish and the Cormorant

'How can we?'

'Don't you worry about a thing,' replied the cormorant. 'I'll take you, one by one, to my special retreat. Only God and I know the way there. It's the most secret place in the world, a little pond made by nature, and never seen by human beings. I'll save you!'

They believed him. So one by one, the fish were carried to that faraway pond under a huge, overhanging rock. The cormorant, that good fellow, placed them there. The pond was clear, shallow, and narrow.

He then caught them, without any trouble, one a day. That's how he taught them, at their expense, not to have confidence in those whose habit it is to eat them.

Some turkeys, threatened by a fox, used a tree for their fortress. The crafty fox went round and round the tree, and noted that all the turkeys were on their guard. He cried out in a rage, 'These birds are making fun of me! Why should they be the only ones who can go against nature? By golly, I won't have it!'

The shining moon, glistening above the tree, seemed to mock him as well.

But he was no fool. In fact, he had a whole bag of terrible tricks at his disposal. First he pretended to leap up the tree, then he played dead, then came to life again. He lifted his tail and waving it deftly, made it glitter in the moonlight, and he performed a hundred other tricks. Harlequin himself couldn't have danced so many roles.

None of the turkeys dared to go to sleep even for an instant. The fox exhausted them by keeping them awake and tense for so long, all concentrated on him. At last, the poor bedazzled turkeys were so bewildered they began to fall out of the tree. As each one fell, the fox seized it and put it to one side.

He got nearly half of them that way, and took them, one by one, off to his larder.

The more you concentrate on the idea of danger, the more likely you are to get defeated by it.

Still, in the end they didn't lose much, since some man would have caught them anyway in due course. What difference does it make who eats you, man, wolf or bird? Any tummy is about the same. A day earlier, a day later, it hardly matters, really.

fox, still young, but cunning, saw a horse for the first time in his life. He ran to his friend the wolf, who was a real innocent, and said, 'Come quick! There's a big, beautiful animal grazing in our field! The very sight of him thrills me!'

The wolf just laughed. 'You think he's stronger than we are? Describe him to me.'

'Oh, if I were an artist I would paint him; if I were a scientist I'd analyse him for you. But I can't. You'll have to see him, to feel the joy I felt. Who knows, he could be a marvellous meal sent to us by Fortune.'

They approached the horse. He was not interested in making such friends, so he got ready to run away.

'Sir,' said the fox, 'your humble servants would like to know your name.'

The horse, who was far from stupid, said, 'You're welcome to read my name. The smith wrote it around my shoe.'

The fox excused himself. 'My parents were unable to teach me to read. They are poor, in fact all they have in the world is the hole they inhabit. Now the wolf, here, his parents are upper class. They gave him a fine education, I'm sure.'

The wolf, flattered by these words, approached the horse proudly. But his vanity cost him four teeth. The horse gave him a sharp kick and ran off. So there lay the wolf, all hurting and sad.

'Brother,' said the fox, 'this situation makes me understand what some clever people once told me. This horse has written on your jawbone that the wise man doesn't trust anything or anyone he doesn't know.'

I wonder why Aesop thinks the fox is so special? He says it's the fox's cunning he admires. Well, I've tried to find out more about the cunning of the fox, and I haven't come up with any evidence for it at all. When the wolf needs to defend himself or attack somebody, doesn't he do as good a job as the fox? I happen to think the wolf is even more intelligent, and I'm not afraid to say so.

However, here's a case where the honour falls to the fox. One night he saw the reflection of the moon at the bottom of a well: its fat, round image looked just like a big cheese. There were two pails in the well, balancing each other on a rope. They were meant to be pulled up and down in turns to draw up the water. The fox, who was dying to get hold of the cheese he saw in the well, got himself into the top pail. Bang, down he went, and up went the empty pail. The fox learned something, but it was a painful lesson and he feared for his life. How was he to get out, unless some other hungry animal came along the path and got charmed by the same image and fell into the same misery?

Two days passed without anyone visiting the well.

Time, which always keeps on moving, during the course of two nights cut a crescent shape through the front of the moon. The fox was getting desperate.

Finally, along came the fox's old friend the wolf, howling. The fox shouted out to him, 'Hey, comrade, I've got good news for you! You see this thing in my well? It's an exquisite cheese. The heavenly cow gave the milk for it, and the gods made it. Jupiter himself, if he were sick, would get better if he tasted the cheese! I've already eaten half of it, as you can see, but I'll let you have the rest. Come on down in the pail. I left it up there specially for you!' The story was pretty thin. The wolf was a fool to believe him. He went down, and his weight made the fox's pail go up again.

But let's not laugh at the wolf. It's easy to believe in what you strongly desire, just as it's easy to believe in what you are afraid of.